'The master of dramatic silhouettes illustrates
the Bible text with fabulous vigour . . .' *The Times*

'Children of all ages will appreciate the visual and verbal
delights of this truly glorious book' *Education*

'A vivid, dramatic quality, ringingly clear and timeless . . .
a treasurable perennial' *Evening Standard*

'The whole thing is truly a work of art. The illustrations,
the print, indeed the whole design is masterly' *Child Education*

'The illustrations show reverence, tenderness and a
sense of humour . . . This is a beautiful modern interpretation
of the Christmas story' *Illustrated London News*

Also by Jan Pieńkowski:
The Fairy Tales

'The quality of an heirloom . . . Pieńkowski has reworked the oldest genre
in the world with the most ancient of skills: real magic' *Guardian*

The First Christmas

The King James Version

with pictures

by

Jan Pieńkowski

PUFFIN

IN THE DAYS of Herod the King, the angel Gabriel was sent from God unto a city named Nazareth, to a virgin espoused to a man whose name was Joseph;

IT CAME to pass that there went out a decree that all the world should be taxed, every one in his own city. And Joseph went up from Nazareth to the city called Bethlehem, to be taxed with Mary his wife, being great with child.

AND SHE brought forth her firstborn son, and wrapped him in swaddling clothes, and laid him in a manger; because there was no room for them in the inn.

There were in the same country shepherds
keeping watch over their flock by night.
And the angel of the Lord came upon them,
and they were sore afraid.

And the angel said unto them, Fear not:
I bring you good tidings of great joy.
For unto you is born a Saviour, which is Christ
the Lord. And this shall be a sign unto you;
ye shall find the babe wrapped in swaddling clothes,
lying in a manger.

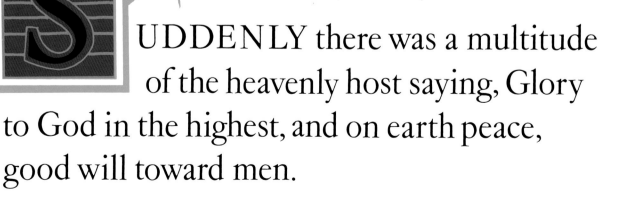

SUDDENLY there was a multitude
of the heavenly host saying, Glory
to God in the highest, and on earth peace,
good will toward men.

THE SHEPHERDS said one to another,
Let us now go to Bethlehem.
And they found Mary, and Joseph, and the babe
lying in a manger.

And all they that heard it wondered at those things which were told them by the shepherds. But Mary kept all these things, and pondered them in her heart.

And the shepherds returned, praising God.

BEHOLD, there came wise men from
the east, saying, Where is he that is
born King of the Jews? For we have seen his star
in the east, and are come to worship him.

When Herod the King heard these things,
he was troubled. And he sent them to Bethlehem,
and said, Go and search diligently for the child;
and when ye have found him, bring me word again,
that I may come and worship him also.

WHEN THEY had heard the King, they departed; and lo, the star went before them, till it stood over where the young child was.

And they saw the young child with Mary
his mother, and fell down and worshipped him;
and when they had opened their treasures,
they presented unto him gifts:
gold, and frankincense, and myrrh.

Being warned in a dream that they should
not return to Herod, they departed into their
own country another way.

AND THE ANGEL appeared
to Joseph in a dream, saying, Arise,
and take the child and his mother, and flee
into Egypt, for Herod will seek the child
to destroy him.

When he arose, he took the child and his mother by night, and departed into Egypt.

THEN HEROD was exceeding wroth, and sent forth and slew all the children that were in Bethlehem, from two years old and under.

Then was there lamentation and weeping and great mourning.

BUT WHEN Herod was dead, an angel
appeared in a dream to Joseph
in Egypt, saying, Take the child and his mother,
and go into the land of Israel: for they are dead
which sought the young child's life.

And he took the child and his mother, and came
into the land of Israel, and dwelt in Nazareth.

ND THE CHILD grew, and waxed
strong in spirit, filled with wisdom:
and the grace of God was upon him.

For my mother and father

Extracts from the Authorized King James Version of the Bible
which is Crown Copyright in England are reproduced by
permission of Eyre & Spottiswoode, Her Majesty's Printers, London.
The words are taken from
Luke 1:5, 26, 27, 30–33, 38; 2:1, 3–5, 7–16, 18–20, 40
Matthew 2:1–3, 8, 9, 11–14, 16, 18–21, 23

The illustrator would like to thank the following for their help:
Rowena Hart, Robert Roper, Hilary Saunders and Jane Walmsley

PUFFIN BOOKS

Published by the Penguin Group: London, New York, Ireland,
Australia, Canada, India, New Zealand and South Africa
Penguin Books Ltd, Registered Offices:
80 Strand, London WC2R 0RL, England

penguin.com

First published by William Heinemann Ltd, 1984
Published in Puffin Books, 1987
Published in this edition, 2006